WELCOME TO
PASSPORT TO READING
A beginning reader's ticket to a brand-new world!

Every book in this program is designed to build read-along and read-alone skills, level by level, through engaging and enriching stories. As the reader turns each page, he or she will become more confident with new vocabulary, sight words, and comprehension.

These PASSPORT TO READING levels will help you choose the perfect book for every reader.

READING TOGETHER
Read short words in simple sentence structures together to begin a reader's journey.

READING OUT LOUD
Encourage developing readers to sound out words in more complex stories with simple vocabulary.

READING INDEPENDENTLY
Newly independent readers gain confidence reading more complex sentences with higher word counts.

READY TO READ MORE
Readers prepare for chapter books with fewer illustrations and longer paragraphs.

This book features sight words from the educator-supported Dolch Sight Words List. This encourages the reader to recognize commonly used vocabulary words, increasing reading speed and fluency.

For more information, please visit lbyr.com/passporttoreading.

Enjoy the journey!

Cover design by Elaine Lopez-Levine. Cover illustration by Artful Doodlers.

Little, Brown and Company
Hachette Book Group
1290 Avenue of the Americas, New York, NY 10104
Visit us at LBYR.com

First Edition: February 2020

Little, Brown and Company is a division of Hachette Book Group, Inc.
The Little, Brown name and logo are trademarks of Hachette Book Group, Inc.

The publisher is not responsible for websites (or their content)
that are not owned by the publisher.

Library of Congress Control Number 2019950357

ISBNs: 978-0-316-45517-6 (pbk.), 978-0-316-43029-6 (Scholastic edition),
978-0-316-45519-0 (ebook), 978-0-316-45533-6 (ebook),
978-0-316-45530-5 (ebook)

Printed in the United States of America

CW

10 9 8 7 6 5 4 3 2 1

Passport to Reading titles are leveled by independent reviewers applying the
standards developed by Irene Fountas and Gay Su Pinnell in *Matching Books
to Readers: Using Leveled Books in Guided Reading*, Heinemann, 1999.

OFFICIAL
MARK OF
SPIRIT

DREAMWORKS

Spirit
RIDING FREE

Spring Beginnings

Adapted by R. J. Cregg

LITTLE, BROWN AND COMPANY
New York   Boston

Attention, Spirit Riding Free fans!
Look for these words
when you read this book.
Can you spot them all?

rears

pregnant

curtsy

waltz

It is springtime in Miradero.
The PALs—Pru, Abigail,
and Lucky—race their
horses across the frontier.

"I will win first
place," Lucky says.
She does!

Their race ends in a valley.
This is where Spirit's herd lives!

The girls walk toward
the wild horses.

A gray horse named Smoke rears
when the PALs reach the herd.

He does not look happy.
He is protecting
something.

The girls see a pregnant mare.
That means the horse is
going to have a baby!

Lucky thinks they should check
on the mare again tomorrow.

Back at Lucky's house,
Aunt Cora has exciting news.

The new governor
is visiting Miradero.
There will be a fancy
ball to welcome him.

All the PALs are invited!
The girls cannot wait to
go to the ball.
They need to get ready.

First, Lucky shows
her friends how to be
graceful on the stairs.
Abigail slips and falls!

Then, Lucky teaches
them how to talk
to the governor.
Pru is so nervous!

The next day, the PALs and
Pru's dad go to the valley.
They will check on
the pregnant mare.

Mr. Granger tries to get to the mare,
but Smoke rears at him, too.

Mr. Granger cannot get
close to the mother horse.

"There is nothing we can do,"
Mr. Granger says.
"She will have her baby
without our help."

Later, the PALs continue
getting ready for the ball.

Aunt Cora teaches them how to curtsy.

She also teaches them how to waltz.

The girls are finally ready for the ball!

Just then, Spirit arrives!

He wants Lucky to follow him.

Something is wrong!

"What about the ball?"
Abigail asks.

The horses are more
important than a ball!
The PALs follow Spirit
as fast as they can!

The friends reach the herd.
The wild horses are upset!
"We have to get to the mare,"
says Lucky.

She walks toward the herd,
but Smoke charges at her.

Spirit stops him and guides
the girls to the mare.

Pru goes to the mother horse.
"She is ready to have
the baby," Pru says.

There is no time to
get Mr. Granger.

The PALs have to help
the mare by themselves!

Boomerang, Spirit, and
Chica Linda stand guard.
Abigail keeps the mare calm.

Pru cannot take care
of the foal alone.
She needs Lucky's help!

Pru and Lucky work together.
The foal is born!

Abigail hugs the baby horse.

"He is the cutest thing I
have ever seen!" she says.

The foal takes his first steps.

He falls down.

Spirit helps him up.

They join the

rest of the herd.

The friends are happy that
the mare and foal are okay.
"That little guy needs a name,"
says Pru.

"I have an idea!" says Abigail.

"I bet it is Sprinkles," Pru guesses.

Lucky asks, "Is it Bunny or Gingersnap?"

"I think it should be Governor!"
says Abigail.

The PALs all agree.

Governor is a perfect name.